RAMBLINGS

FROM A

BROKEN MIND

POETRY & SHORT STORIES

GIANNI FRANCO

ISBN-13: 9781736621745 (paperback)
ISBN-13: 9781736621738 (e-book)
ISBN-13: 9781736621752 (hardcover)

Cover Art by Gianni Franco
Library of Congress Control Number: 2021920320
First Edition, Printed in the United States of America.

The mind disperses thoughts like grains of sand sailing within the wind. We hope they form sandcastles when they land to then disintegrate into the sea.

Gianni Franco

A Dollar and a Dream

"Dottie. We need to meet. I have something important to tell you."

The Florida sun beamed through the window, melting the vanilla ice cream topped with chocolate flakes, which the waitress had delivered to Dottie a few minutes prior. Loving Life Café in Fort Myers offered the most aromatic coffee in the city, perhaps the State; the beans delivered weekly from Jamaica and ground for every cup. For thirty years they'd known each other and never once did they add cream or sugar, but on occasion a dribble or a pour of liquor spiked the java.

"So, what's so important, Jerry *Yorkshire*. I've always loved that last name of yours. Anyway, are you dying or something?" She spooned the creamy liquid from the dish and slurped.

"Not yet, Dottie *Doolittle*. Good thing because I wish I could live forever."

"If you're asking me to grant you that option, I don't have the power to allow it. Are you on one of your tangents again?"

"No. I need more time and really need to live forever. I have so much more to accomplish."

"Oh, honey… Jerry. We're in our seventies. Eighty is just around the corner. It's best to have drinks and enjoy whatever time we have remaining instead of pondering the impossible."

"But, I have ideas and goals I need to reach."

"Oh… my foolish, old Jerry. We all do. You're such a prima donna."

"Come on, Dottie. I'm writing two fiction novels and a memoir. How am I supposed to finish all the work with a finite timeline?"

"Well… perhaps you shouldn't have wasted all your living years. It's not like you didn't have the time available to you. I must say it's almost as if you were lazy and now are crying wolf."

"That's offensive, Miss Dottie. Such insinuations are vile," he shouted, gritting his teeth and pounding the table with a fist.

"Now, now, Jerry. Stop acting like a child who can't have his cookie. You should've been more resilient like myself. Three husbands, four children and I still had time to write three novels and two chapbooks. What's your excuse?"

"Those books weren't even that good."

"Oh, my… the Amazon ratings and sales state otherwise. Is there anything else you need to tell me?"

"Nope. But—"

"I think we've reached the end of our coffee date. Well, good luck with all your writing goals. Thank you for the coffee and the milkshake in a bowl. Let's meet next month or whenever."

"Yes, we will unless my wish comes true."

Dottie sipped the last of her coffee and sighed. She tapped the table and smirked, then strutted from the café and into her Maserati. Jerry ogled her every move while wondering why she never believed in his aspirations. "I still wish to live forever," he mumbled, spinning the mug from hand to hand. He slid twenty dollars under the saucer and dawdled to the door humming, waiting for her to leave before venturing outside. He didn't own a fancy car nor did he drive often, promenading to the bars and grocers while checking the Fitbit and smiling as the steps accumulated.

The unpredictable Florida weather showed its hand. He shuddered at the bolt of lightning and thunder; a shelf cloud approaching with fury. Hoping to evade a calamity, he veered onto an unfrequented trail, a shortcut he had used one time many years ago. Tramping between the tall grass and shrubbery, his foot snagged a vine. He crashed onto his knees, losing consciousness for a moment. As his vision refocused, a man appeared just ahead of him. Dressed in camouflage, he sat with his back against a tree and legs extended.

He swigged a flask, then smirked. "Can you spare some change?"

Jerry blinked, then knuckled his eyes to confirm this wasn't a Floridian mirage. "I'd worry more about the storm than money. You need to move somewhere safe and not next to a tree. It's a rule unless you want to be struck by lightning."

The man chortled and lit a cigarette. "Storms are nothing. Bombs and bullets scare me. I've done three tours in the deserts and jungles to return to live among the weeds. Want a sip or a smoke?"

"No. I'm all set. Sorry about your misfortune," he said dispirited.

"Apologies nor thoughts and prayers will fix my situation. The country gave up on me, sending me to the woods. A lucky lightning strike would help me. How about some change?"

Jerry patted his pockets. "I don't have any."

"Of course you do."

"I really don't. I just paid for me and my friend at the café. She left me with the bill and walked out."

"What a shame. Look, man, you have money for me deep within your pocket."

"You're a comic and a veteran?" Jerry chuckled.

"I happen to be all-knowing. I heard about your wish."

"My what?" Shocked, he lost his breath for a moment, almost fainting. "A wish? We've never spoken."

"I know all. Now, give me your last dollar and I'll help with the wish."

"I don't have any more money."

"Check them one more time."

"Fine. I'll oblige your magic trick." With a pompous grin, Jerry dug into his pockets and found a crumpled bill. "What the hell?" he said marveled.

"I'll take that. Please." He handed the money to the man. "Thank you, Jerry. I can make your wish come true." A sly smile separated his thick, unkempt beard.

"Really? And how will you accomplish that feat?"

"Just as I did with your donation. I might be homeless, but I have powers as well. If you trust me, I'll let you know where to go." He straightened the dollar between his frail fingers.

"Tell me." He inched closer to the man.

"I will, sir, but please step back and be kind."

Jerry obliged. "Please. And, may I have *your* name?"

"A name?" He stroked his beard. "Jeremiah. Last names are of no use to either of us." He gulped from the flask. "Listen carefully. Go to 1313 Main Street. At midnight the wooden door will glow red. Open it with care, making certain not to disturb the carvings of the Greek drama masks overhead. Once inside, your wish will be granted."

"So, I just go to a door and walk inside? What's the catch?"

"The catch is that once you're through those doors, we make the rules, but I can assure you that you'll live forever."

"Fine. I'll think about it."

"Thank you for your donation, sir. And, be careful with that alligator creeping up on you." He pointed at the trail. Frantic, Jerry spun and searched the path.

"There's nothing there, Jeremiah. Why are you playing games?" No response arrived. He turned to confront him. "What the hell?" he said shaking his head. The man in camouflage had disappeared.

Jerry debated throughout the evening, at times yelling at his reflection in the mirror. The hope of living forever outweighing any of the lingering uncertainty. Within minutes from midnight, he found himself at the door. To his astonishment, it changed from brown to bright red. *Go on. Do it.* He turned the handle. As it opened, the hinges creaked. The Greek masks remained stationary, but their eyes beamed blue. Jerry avoided any eye contact and continued straight ahead.

He came upon a mirror hovering mid-air. A quick glance, then a double take. He refused to believe its existence as he traced the image on the glass. His face and body had reverted into someone he yearned for, his twenty-year-old self. In the distance, neighing horses striped with rainbows galloped upon a carousel against a backdrop of oceans, mountains, and wetlands.

"Glad you made it, Jerry. Jeremiah was certain you'd arrive. Hop on a friendly steed if you'd like. The views are amazing," he said with a hearty voice.

"Who or what are you? Where are you?" he shouted.

"I am everything and nothing. I am here and there. I am the puppeteer of the Universe. I am the dark matter. You may refer to me as Tenebris."

"I don't know. I think I should leave," Jerry stuttered while backing away.

"You may not. Once you enter, you may never leave."

"This must be a joke for a television show. Where are the cameras?"

"None exist. You are for me to view and control."

"I didn't sign up for this. Let me go. This isn't fair."

"But it is. Your wish has been granted. You now have all the time you need to address your dreams. If you leave the premises, you'll return to that old version of yourself that no one wants, not even you."

"Fair enough. Will you do me one favor?"

"And, what is that?"

"Show yourself to me, Tenebris."

"I'm standing ahead of you, but because you are human you cannot comprehend my essence. Let's begin our time together and forget this gibberish you ask of me."

Once more, Jerry glanced at the mirror holding his youthfulness, gazing at himself for several minutes, then smiling with surety.

"Fine. What do I, or we, do now?"

"Glad you've agreed to move on, Jerry. I knew you would. It's difficult avoiding the beautiful, younger version of oneself. Here's how this will work, of which you have no say. I am now your master. I'll allot time for you to write daily, but the amount is based on how much manure you shovel. If the horses and carousel is to my liking, then all will be well. If not, you'll continue to labor until I say you can quit."

Jerry had turned to his juvenile reflection, ignoring all of what his master had said. Hours would pass before he relinquished the mesmerism. By that time, the mounds the horses had accumulated rose well over ten feet, thus the subsequent weeks offered no time to write. Jerry hopes one day he'll be able to overcome his workload.

A Cigarette, a Smile and a Squirrel

Anima had been sick for months, bedridden by cirrhosis, which had progressed to Stage 4, otherwise known as end-stage liver disease. Her daughter, Bella, visited daily to keep her company and clean the home. She knew once Mom passed, hopefully in peace or not, the ending irrelevant; she'd inherit the condo and not have to pay rent anymore nor deal with the bickering.

Bella Buttoni unlocked the front door, and just as she traversed the entrance, Anima's hand-bell rang. "You're late again. Those mental pills you keep taking are going to be the death of me and you. I need your help. Come to me. Now." The bell continued without pause.

Bella dropped her oversized, fake Gucci purse on the couch and sprinted to Anima's room. "I'm here now. What is it, Mom? What can I do? I'm sorry I took so long. Are you ok?"

"No. Don't you care about me anymore? Did you forget about me? I'm dying."

"I do care Mom and you're not dying." A necessary lie to tell a dying human. "Do you have any pain?" she asked, tucking the bedsheet under the latex mattress of the hospital bed.

"The pain's all over," she said, pointing her frail, bluing fingers towards her swollen, yellow toes poking from the blanket. "Why can't you breathe, Bella? Do you have the cancer?"

Bella sighed. "No, Mom. I ran to your room and I'm out of breath."

"Are you sure you don't have the cancer? Maybe you caught it from me or one of your boyfriends."

"No, Mom. Cancer is *not* contagious and you don't have it." Another lie. The doctor had told Bella the blood tests pointed to cancer developing soon. "What can I do for you?"

"Nothing. I just wanted to say hi," she said with a sly grin.

"Come on. Give me a damn break. I ran because I thought something was seriously wrong with you. Call me *only* when it's urgent. Can you remember that for me? Please…"

Anima paused for several moments and searched the room. "Remember? You should remember. You're such a brat, Bella. I've done everything for you. Birthed and bathed you. I helped you with your first period and taught you how to have sex with that loser Greg from high school. You're unworthy to be in my room. Get out."

"Come on, Mom. You're just being ridiculous now."

"Get out." She struggled for a breath. Not too long ago, she roared commands like a drill sergeant, but adding to the cirrhosis, emphysema had engulfed her lungs. "Be gone."

"Fine. I'm sure I'll be back when you start ringing that stupid bell again."

Bella stormed to the kitchen and retrieved a bottle of scotch from the cupboard, filling a tall glass. A quick sip helped swallow three Xanax pills. She ambled towards the only window in the unit. One hand slid it open while the other pulled out a pack of cigarettes.

She chased each drag with two gulps. With the glass emptied, she laid the smoldering cigarette on the sun-bleached sill, adding to the trail of charred imprints resembling railroad tracks. She refilled the glass and returned to the open window and lit another.

As she inhaled the first drag, the bell rang again. "What are you doing out there? I smell smoke. You can't do that here. I'm dying. Put it out. Now."

"Oh my god, Mom. I'm not smoking. Can you just leave me alone for one goddam second?"

Turning, Bella stared into the concrete yard, barren except for one elm tree, which gave her serenity when she visited. As she brought the glass to her pursed lips, a white-tailed squirrel bounced from branch to branch beckoning her attention. "Aren't you the cutest little thing," she said, extending her arm far enough out the window to keep the smoke at bay. As the elixir took hold she slipped into a dream, joining the springing squirrel on the tree elevator.

Anima slithered onto the edge of the bed, her legs wobbling like stilts as she gripped the walker and rose to her feet. Taking the first step proved futile as the oxygen tentacles yanked her back onto the bed. She ripped the rigid inserts from her nose, throwing them to the floor. She rose once again, latching onto the curved handles with a determined grip, her twisting knuckles yearning to break through the diaphanous skin. Her eyes bobbed with each lurching step, as the worn tennis balls at the base of the walker scraped the floor. "Almost there," she mumbled, as her shoulders bumped the hallway walls.

Meanwhile, Bella had fallen deeper into reverie. She and the squirrel had become best of friends, propped on a branch and sharing the remnants of a walnut. "I love you so much," she said, rubbing her tail, "I wish Mom was more like you." The squirrel offered a subtle nod while munching.

Anima reached the kitchen swaying and gasping. Leaning against the black, marble countertop she exchanged the walker for a tug of the top drawer. The steel utensils crashed and clanged. Her vision had faded at the same rate as her body, but her memory remained intact. Searching through the drawer, she located the largest tool from the bunch. "This will do," she said, lunging towards the walker and resuming her shuffle through the condo.

Bella's heart warmed as she entertained the endless possibilities of a fulfilling life, if only the squirrel would stay with her, love her as no one had.

Plodding, Anima made it across the tiled floor. As she came upon Bella, one hand steadied the walker, while the other raised the eight-inch butcher knife above her head. With one swift thrust, she pierced the center of Bella's back. Bella collapsed, her body splayed atop the window sill. "I love you, too," said the squirrel as they nuzzled noses on the edge of the branch. Bella gurgled a final breath with a bloodied smile, several droplets extinguishing the cigarette upon the ledge. Anima collapsed forward, snapping the blade's handle as it tore through Bella's back and into Anima's chest. "I told you I was dying, you little, ungrateful, rude brat," she said with a devious smirk and cackle.

September (2014)

Only a few months have passed,
Since bursting buds broke free from frozen soil,
Blossoms bloomed, stretching
Towards the welcoming sun,
The cool winds of spring
Surrendering to the warmth of summer.

The rainbow palette of life
Painted on Earth's canvas,
But only for a blip in time
As Nature has other plans,
Restraining the light for life,
Dissipating jouissance,
The gauntlet of the living unresolved,
Subject to the steely thrashing from the solstice hammer.

The inexorable Universe
Adjudicates existence
The blooms no more, breaths removed,
Yellow, purple, green, blue,
Constricted, frail, folding, faltering
Into the void of the chilling earth,

Gold, brown, orange, black,
The present, future, past,
Obligatory surrender,
What remains are only memories,
September.

The Prowess of Love

Love,
Peaceful like summer dawn,
Alluring as the dew
Slithering upon the erect petal integument,
Passionflower tendrils wane,
Subtle breaths sway their slender ringlets,
Bumblebees siphon nectar,
A raindrop curls the leaf tip,
The liaison soon producing the aromatic fruit.

Love,
The whispers of wind welcome dusk,
Lacrimating whirs fill the spaces
Between the spuming ebb and flow of the sea,
As night accepts the new moon
An occulted star pleads to be seen,
Pulsating, gleaming, beaming,
Methodic and unrelenting,
It seeks pleasure and approval.

Love,
Ordained,
Besought by all,
Denied to some,
Love, an eternal cataclysmic bliss.

Nuanced Coital

The lambskin covering
Of your drum
Beats a spastic rhythm,
Stretching   Quivering.

Our bodies
A turbulent storm
Commanding
The swelling waves.

We impel the other onto
Undiscovered lands,
Then thrust ourselves
Into a maelstrom.

Lips curling,
Flexing   Fellating,
Peeling the rind,
Exposing the fruit,
Swallowing the juice.

Chests
Expanding   Contracting,
Suffocating pleasure,
Weeping   Howling,
Panting,
Writhing torsos,
Sweltering skin,
Felicific virgin screams.

Etiolating,
Whispers fade to silence.

A brief slumber
Before we commence once more.

Justina

The phone vibrated, transitioning to "Born this Way" by Lady Gaga. From a contorted positon, she slid her tingling fingers from under the pillow, extending them to the nightstand and silencing the alarm after several erratic, limp taps. Her mornings always began in this fashion, albeit using the snooze option and having Mom scream to finalize the waking process. Even with all those measures in place, she arrived to her homeroom check-in late. Being a sophomore in high school isn't easy and teachers never understood that not everyone is a morning person. Today, a Saturday, she opted for an afternoon nap, wanting to be well rested for her evening date.

She knuckled her eyes, pressing away the caked remnants from sleep, then stretched, pointing her feet towards the end of the bed and her arms to the ceiling. The amassed tension relieved via a series of pops as she twisted her neck and back. She snapped the bed sheet from her legs and swung them to the edge of the queen pillow-top.

Snaking her toes atop the shag carpet, she searched for the frilly, pink slippers with the butterfly bows. Fate had brought her these loafers not too long ago, perhaps a supernatural divination for the teen. Although addressed to Mom, she ripped open the box delivered by Amazon. Caressing them, she fell in love, then like a responsible child, repackaged them and brought them to her. A day or two later and they disappeared. Mom groaned and growled when questioned. Justina had searched throughout the home with no luck, then one morning she received their exact location.

"Why did you buy me those stupid slippers, Bev?" Bev is what Mom called Grandma when mad at her, which seemed to be quite frequent. The children always used Nana. "You know I hate bows and can't stand butterflies or fuchsia. Bev, the next time you buy me something, you better ask first. I don't need more of this crap. I threw them in the trash."

Justina dashed to the refuse bin just as the rubbish truck arrived at their curb and fished them out, ignoring the loud warnings from the garbage collectors. She stuffed them up her shirt and hurried into the house.

Mom continued her tirade as Justina continued the trek upstairs, yanking the slippers from under her shirt at the last step. Stopping at the bedroom door, she regarded them tight within her grip; one part of her confused, the other disappointed. The nerve to throw away such works of art by people like Mom must be a crime. She hoped the fashion police would arrive one day and arrest her.

She couldn't wait to see if the slippers fit as the bedroom door closed behind her. She figured they would but needed to be certain, plus the exhilaration of trying something new always had its perks. They swaddled her feet like a mound of cotton balls layered with feathers; the fit snug but not too tight.

Today, no different as the day she found them. As her footing firmed against the carpet, she rose nude and ambled towards the full-length, oval mirror. The sun, gleaming through the Venetian blinds, refracted against the reflective glass, jarring her vision with each glance. Blinded and with an outstretched arm she staggered, grasping air and bumping the wall, before snagging and twisting the wand that commanded the sheers to roll like eyelids ready for sleep. She turned on the balls of her feet with delicate precision and reentered the space across the mirror.

She slid a hand up her thigh, then stroked her abdomen, tracing the end of her short journey with careful circles around the cusp of her navel.

"I *am* beautiful, no matter what they say."

Blushing cheeks rose exposing simple dimples as she scanned her image. The reflection vibrant, stunning, soothing, and filled with a love that should never be broken. The pink slippers came into view, and within them, each turquoise toe curled and twisted to peek a clearer view of themselves.

With one swift motion, she spun and skated to the plush stool sitting across from a nightstand turned makeup table, which held a wire loop vanity given to her by Nana as a "secret" birthday gift. On one side of the mirror sat a blue purse filled with an array of cosmetics, which she dug from the trash as well. Mom's reasoning for this throwaway: she didn't like the shade of blue or its white stripes. Nana received an earful during that call too.

She unzipped the bag and retrieved the eyeliner. With the accuracy of a surgeon, she etched the edges of her eyelids with the black wax. Next came the firm bristles from the mascara brush of the same hue. The tarred wand glued itself to her eyelashes curling them to her eyebrows.

Nana always says, "You need to blink or wink to appreciate the look." After blinking a few times, the reflection in the mirror appeased her with accomplishment. Nana was right and the most important thing Nana said after that was to make certain to add color. "If you don't have color, then you won't get love."

Next, the eyeshadow palette and lipstick. She brushed crimson and violet above her eyelids, painting like Picasso or Matisse, followed by a merlot lipstick. She grabbed a tissue and moistened it with her tongue, then sponged away any imperfections, which were few.

"I need two more things to complete me." She rose from the stool and marched to the small closet lined with so many clothes pressing against each other none of them needed ironing. Hanging in the corner, beyond the jackets, jeans, and suits, hung a blue dress embroidered with silhouettes of butterflies and flowers. She loved the outfit, but Nana didn't gift this one. Justina had purchased it for two dollars from the Treasure Trove, a local thrift shop. The fashion police needed to pay the store a visit as well because it was worth at least thirty dollars even with the missing designer tag.

She donned the silk ensemble, then rummaged the stacked shoe boxes, sending the sneakers, loafers, and boots cartwheeling to the floor. Frenzied, she couldn't find her most prized possessions. Hopefully, Mom hadn't discovered her secret and thrown those out too. "There you are, my beauties." She beamed as she pulled the last carton from the rear corner of the closet. She had rushed to hide them one day when Mom wouldn't stop banging on her door and screaming to come out and talk about Nana. She contemplated the black stilettos with the red bottoms within her clutch, then slipped them on. They hugged her feet like Nana's gentle embrace and those red soles designated her queen.

"I *am* beautiful, no matter what they say," she said mesmerized by the reflection ahead of the tall mirror.

A weak tap at the door turned into an annoying barrage of thwacks, awaking her from the trance.

"Justin. Justin! It's time to get ready. Your girlfriend's here for your movie date tonight."

"Okay," he replied, pitched higher than normal.

"What'd you say, Justin?"

"Okay. I'll be ready in a few minutes," he barked. The hardest part of the day lay ahead as he rushed to remove the dress, heels, and makeup but not before one last glance at the mirror.

"I *am* beautiful, no matter what they say."

Holed House

Cletus and Jeb had surveilled the house on Foggia Avenue in Lehigh Acres for weeks, sopping the vinyl seats of their pickup truck under the Florida sun. They confirmed the property to be abandoned and decided to make their move, unloading the equipment from the tonneau and entering the abode by jimmying the lock on the back door.

"Jeb, this *Florida Moonshine* is gonna be awesome. We're gonna be rich," he said with a Southern drawl.

"You know it. I've waited my whole life for this opportunity. Let's get 'er done."

They assembled the components of the distillery with unbridled fervor: a fifty-gallon, copper pot, clamps, hoses, condenser, and burner.

"Jeb, make sure all the pieces for the mountain dew are tight. Don't mess it up. We got one shot to get this process started. After the first run, everything will be as smooth as molasses. We'll winnow out all the producers and become the kings of Southwest Florida."

"I'm on it, Cletus. I'm excited. Never thought this day would come. I just have a few more bolts to tighten and a couple hoses to attach. Then, we're ready to fire it up."

Cletus finished the work while Jeb loaded the pot with mash, then lit a cigarette and sat on the dirt floor.

"Good to go," Jeb said grinning. "Light it up."

"Alright, bud. I'm ready."

He extinguished the butt under his boot and lit the burner. They watched in awe as the contents boiled and bubbled; the white lightning dripping into the collection cup.

"Like magic, Jeb. I can already see the dollar bills filling this house."

"You got that right. Rich is as rich does, Cletus. A few more days and we'll start bottling the hooch."

They stepped away from the still and leaned against the far wall. Cletus retrieved a flask from his overalls and swigged, then passed it to Jeb. They smirked at each other and nodded. An hour later an explosion jolted them from their doze.

"What the hell? Jeb, what just happened?"

"I don't know." He pointed at the wall. "It's gone," he said awed.

"I'm well aware. I'm standing next to you. The still is destroyed. What did you do wrong? What are we gonna do with a holed house? Go check your work. Now!"

Fidgeting, Jeb checked the contraption. "I found the problem, Cletus. The pressure valve never opened. I don't know if it's the wrong size for this still or if it was just stuck."

"Incredible. A stupid valve and a holed house. Neither good for anything. You should've checked it, Jeb. I told you to make sure everything was proper. Anyway—"

"I think I hear sirens, Cletus," he said with a shaky voice.

"We better get a move on before someone shows up. Quick, grab what's left of the equipment and load it onto the truck. We'll find another place. No way am I giving up on this *Florida Moonshine*."

Angel (1999)

Innocence,
Designed for you,
Patience and Purity,
Sought only through you

Your eyes reflect from the sea,
Hazel as the sand rounding my knees,
Like a statue I rise seeking their view,
To then be imbued with quietude

You whisper like the uninhabited shells of the sea
"Stay strong, there is eternity."
I bow with uncertainty
"There is no peace."

You caress my cheek
With an ocean breeze,
Redolent lavender you breathe,
Soothing the remnants of my soul

With my demise near, you provide prudent reprieve.
I now know
You are my Angel.
For You,
I devote perpetual adulation.

Flesh to Stone

Somber and silent, the Palmer family dawdled to the burial plot. Shannon, their daughter, had passed away the prior year from breast cancer at age twenty-five. Eileen, her mother, carried twenty-six roses to lay at her grave while Brett, her father, held a box filled with the same number of candles. Cake would not be served.

"Hey, Danny. Look. They've come back," she said, perched on one end of the headstone.

"What do you want, Emily? Don't you see I'm busy praying?"

"Yes, I'm aware. It's not the first time you've told me. And, don't be snippy with me."

"Fine. I'm sorry, but if you haven't noticed, I can't do anything else. Same stance, day in, day out. Anyway… who's here?"

"It's the Palmers. They've come to visit us once more. It's so nice we're in their thoughts in our time of need."

"Try to get their attention again. Maybe they'll be able to get us out of here," Danny said. "How many times is a charm?"

"What does that even mean?"

"Never mind."

Their concrete prisons came to be in a most peculiar way. Under a fiery harvest moon, Emily and Danny arrived at the cemetery to explore the paranormal tales their teenage classmates had supposedly experienced. Danny thought their friends watched too many vampire movies, but Emily, unswayed by his outlandish rebukes, knew someone or something lived amongst the thousands of entombed bodies.

"Quick. Come over here. I think I see something," Emily said, following the zigzagging flashlight around the granite nametags.

"I can't. It's too dark. I think this is a waste of time. Let's go back to the car. I'd rather be home watching a movie instead of running around this hellhole." He had forgotten his torch in the car and trailed Emily by several yards, bumping into headstones and slipping into divots.

"I see it. There. Up ahead. The shimmering. Do you see it, Danny? Next to the elm tree. I've almost reached it."

The iridescence hovered, then zipped into the night sky, dove through the ground, and reappeared at eye level. She stretched a hand, but it evaded her attempts.

Impatient, she shouted, "Come on, ghost, or whatever you are. Let me touch you."

It rose once more, this time as high as the moon, returning like a falling star, stopping just above Emily's head and said, "If I let you touch me, will you deal with the consequences?"

"Depends. What kind?"

"That is for me to know and you to find out." The being grinned and rubbed its translucent hands together.

Danny had finally caught up to Emily. Panting with eyes wide, he said, "What the... What is that thing?"

"It's our new friend. It wants me to touch it. It'll be fine, if we do it."

"I don't think *we* should be placing our fingers into some floating thing that changes colors. Let's go back to the car and go home. Like fast."

Emily centered the flashlight against her chest, illuminating her chin. "No, Danny. Stay and be a good boyfriend. We'll graze it. Everything will be fine. I promise."

"What has happened to your face?"

Her skin alternated between crimson and white as her cheekbones ballooned and rose above her brow. Her usual timid smile now extended from ear to ear as if it had been carved into her skull. He thought disfigurations such as these only occurred with a talented makeup artist. A tingle soon followed, creeping along his spine and scalp.

"This is not a good idea, Emily." He shuddered, knuckling his eyes.

"Give me your hand. Now, dammit!"

Exasperated, he held his breath, hoping she'd change her mind, then as he blinked, her face returned to normal. "Okay," he said, exhaling with a deep groan.

They walked towards the being, straining to reach it with outstretched hands. Upon contact, it enveloped their fingers with hot air. Jolted, they jumped backwards. The being morphed into human form, standing as tall as the elm. A wicked grin exposed razors and fangs lining his mouth, dribbling blood onto an untamed, white beard.

"My name is Belial. Ego lapis projeci te. You are now banished to the world of immobile cherubs, to sit forever more and guard this property, or until I decide otherwise. Be gone."

Belial snapped his fingers and banished the teens to their stone prison. Danny, in the prayer stance, and Emily, the eternal harpist. The police searched the cemetery to no avail, walking past the monument several times.

"Play your harp louder for the Palmers," Danny pleaded as Eileen approached, kneeling beside Emily.

"Aren't these cherubs just the cutest, Brett?"

"Yes, love. They're just as wonderful as they are sad. A little weird since we never ordered that option with the gravestone."

"Oh, I know. I think someone in the front office understood our pain with losing a child and decided to add these angels for our Shannon. It's good she has company when we're not here."

"I guess nice people doing good things still exist."

"They sure do. I'm going to clean them up a bit." She retrieved a handkerchief from her purse and dusted Emily.

"Stop touching me, Miss Palmer. Don't you see I'm trying to strum? Dammit, Danny. She's not listening."

"Oh… Eileen. You've hit the perfect spot. Keep going. Don't stop. I like it. Dammit, Emily. She stopped."

"There we go, Brett. They're all clean now. Next time, we should bring a brush and an organic cleaning solution. Get these two cuties shining like the stars."

"Great idea, love. Let's head out. We'll be back soon enough."

"Oh, brother… They want to scrub us down. I think that's going to hurt, or maybe feel good for you. Someday we'll get out of here and get back to our normal lives," Emily said, plucking the strings with all her strength.

"I can only hope. Genuflecting all the time hurts."

"I love you," Emily said.

"I love you too. I can't wait to get a kiss."

"How do you know you're going to get a kiss?"

"Well, I do pray every day."

"Hopefully, if your prayers are answered, I'll give you a great big smooch. I miss holding hands."

They hope the Palmers will be able to release them from their misery, but hope is not for the pusillanimous. The case remains open as the police continue exploring every option, pleading for information from the public during their monthly pressers.

The Millennium (1999)

Two thousand years,
Hundreds of generations
Succeeding the one before last

They await the advent of a new era,
Yet, Time fleets,
Capitulating at the behest of Khronos,

Poised Gargoyles escort day to night,
Ensuring what lies ahead
Is nothing short of blight,

The chalk sphere
Sketched on the blackboard sky,
Takes death, gives life

Oh, Midnight Millennium Moon,
Warn the contemporaries,
From the Far West
To the distant Eastern shores,
That Khronos wields his scythe with no remorse.

Best Man Speech (2017, unedited, except for names.)

Now that you have become accustomed to Gianni's different look I can begin.

I am completely flattered to be your best man. I can honestly tell you I did not expect you to ask me. You have many more friends that may have fit the best man position better than I. I said yes because you asked me. How could I say no? We did grow up together. We did do a lot of things together. We skated in our basements on ice made of talcum powder and skates made of socks. We listened to our first songs together when we borrowed albums from Mario's bedroom. Led Zeppelin and Black Sabbath. We crashed cars at 100 mph and walked away alive. We hit 152 mph that day in Wheatland and I made the paper for the wrong reason. We climbed a flag pole to steal an American flag. Wait. I actually did that at the Mapledale Party House. Jim watched from below and left when I got stuck on the roof and then I ended up jumping a full story. So now you have the answer to the mystery as to why the flag disappeared one day from the Mapledale in 1990s and wasn't replaced for 10 years.

Moving on from that, we are here today because the butterfly effect brought us here. We have all had our ups and downs in life and those ups and downs bring us to take certain paths in life. It's a complicated theory. In short, the butterfly effect explains our movements and situations within our lives that brings us to or away from our current destinations. In essence, if a movement or change occurs by anyone or anything in a specific time period it will bring us together or apart in our lives. You can see me for a more in-depth explanation. Those paths of life led Jim and Kate to meet, date, and now are married.

Elise was another part of the butterfly effect. Elise was given to Kate and Jim to allow their bond to grow stronger. Elise, I can assure you that Jim and Kate love you very much and will always do everything and anything they can possibly do for you to make you succeed. Elise, you are their anchor. I believe all of you will agree. When your child or children were born they became your end all be all and thus your anchor to ground you for life. You all have become parents, grandparents, uncles, nieces, nephews, brothers, and sisters at some point in time and that family bond has grounded you to the reality of love and life.

On a more solemn note let us reflect on the people that we have lost. We have lost family members and friends who would have been happy to be here tonight. They will always be in our hearts and minds. We cannot change the past. We can look to the future. The future includes three important people that are here tonight. They do not have to be our best friends or family but they are each other's best friends and family, Kate, Jim and Elise.

We all congratulate you both, Kate and Jim. We all wish you the best for the rest of your lives together. Cheers to you, Kate and Jim, and cheers to all the married couples that are here tonight.

Three Haikus

The summer sun burns
dark shadows onto the skin
drips of sweat on chin

Irma and Harvey
brought heavy rain winds and pain
in the end, love reigned

Christmas . . . red white green
gifts you will always receive
if you are not mean

A Mother's Dying Breath

Early morning on September 9 in Rochester, New York. The leaves on the trees had surrendered their jovial green to autumn's overbearing orange. The sliding glass overlooking the patio and lush lawn remained closed due to the cold, bustling wind.

The living room, with white walls and a matching tile floor, had always resembled a hospital room, and within the last thirty days it couldn't be more apparent. The silence interrupted by a clicking ventilator, signaling the oxygen canister had depleted; it hummed to refill its breath. An oscillating fan buzzed, swirling the pungent urine, vinyl, and latex throughout the home.

Mom, Lidia to most, frail and motionless in a morphine trance atop the grey, vinyl mattress fitted for the portable bedframe on loan from the hospital. The bulky contraption like an adult crib with tall rails preventing her escape, just as the smaller version did when she was a baby.

Only a month ago, Lidia was walking, talking, and feeding herself. She'd carry on with Raquel, the visiting nurse dressed in a yellow dress and bright blue name tag, who came twice a week to assist us and check her vitals. She always announced the numbers aloud with hesitation and drab, then scribbled the results onto a notepad.

"120 over 80. Temperature: 98. Pulse: 65. Glucose: 80. All looks good today," she'd say with an apprehensive smile.

"Good to know. Thank you, Raquel. How long before things change or do you think she'll get better?" I said with a raised brow.

"No. Medical miracles aren't plausible. That being said, everyone's different. She could be good today, but tomorrow can be a completely different scenario. Typically, health inches downward rather than all at once. To be honest with you, I don't think she'll ever be fine. You have to be ready for the change. One thing that's certain is you can never predict the exact day or hour."

"Thanks for the advice and information. I'll monitor her as best I can. I really wish I was a doctor or a nurse. I could take care of her better."

"There's nothing you nor anyone else can do. She's on her own now. I've seen all types of sick people and they're all different. I can assure you that when things start to change with Lidia you'll know."

Raquel paused for a moment, fixating on the chirping birds fluttering about the patio. I hoped her next statement would be positive, but it was not.

"I have some bad news for you. I'll no longer be coming to check Lidia's vitals. Home hospice has been cancelled and will no longer pay for services. All future care is to be rendered in the home by her guardian. That individual is you."

"Why? I don't understand. I need you here to help me," I pleaded.

"Unfortunately, Lidia's vitals no longer need to be documented. She's reached the point of no return. You'll be fine. Just make her comfortable and keep her hospital bed facing the window for sunlight. Stay strong and don't be afraid to give her more morphine. You can adjust the amount higher as the need arises."

I shook my head and shouted, "Is that your last piece of advice for me? Morphine and stay strong?" She didn't appreciate my sarcasm or outburst.

Raquel leered, grabbed her medical bag, and headed towards the door. She turned before exiting. "Yes," she said, then departed.

The door shut. I sighed and sat next to Mom with my hands cupping my face. I shouldn't have been upset with Raquel. She's a nurse doing her job, which she had done for hundreds of deaths before Lidia. I had bestowed upon myself a false friendship with Raquel because I envied her strength and hoped she could cure my mom and resolve my internal turmoil. Raquel had been my only outlet to the outside world because friendships are fleeting.

I held my tears and firmed my voice. "I'll do my best, Mom. We don't need Raquel or anyone."

"Don't you worry. When we die, we die alone. Thank you for all you've done, especially since we've been estranged for most of our lives." That was her last coherent statement of which I had no response.

Today, I gazed at Mom's mottled face and bawled. "Why did you do this to me? Why did you do this now?" I hoped for a mumble or a word, but neither arrived. I hung my head and closed my eyes.

Each hour that passed more difficult than the prior. The downward slope had transitioned into a slalom race. I grabbed the morphine bottle the hospital had provided and attempted to relieve her and myself of our pain, dabbing copious amounts into her mouth. The overdose never arrived.

Out of regret for my attempt, I sprinted between the bathroom and the living room delivering towel compresses to cool her forehead. I had created a myth that cold water would bring her back and absolve my sins, but in reality she could no longer feel and my penance unattainable. Just another pathetic action to comfort her. I held her hand. Horrified by the gelidity, I let go.

Within hours, Lidia's breathing changed for the worse as well; each cycle of a single breath included a minute interval. I lifted her torso, hoping to help her breathe, but in the process multiple ribs snapped against her skin and thumped my palm. I lowered her onto the bed with care and covered her body with a blanket. Weary, I sat and within minutes dozed.

She awoke me with the death growl, a guttural suffocation reverberating throughout the home, shaking her sternum as well as my eardrums. I didn't know what to do. More morphine, more compresses, less breathing, louder grumbling. The thought had crossed my mind to suffocate her with a pillow to stop our misery, but I refrained. A murder charge, although euthanasic, would be unforgivable legally and possibly morally. Anxious, I headed to the kitchen and retrieved a bottle of vodka from the cupboard and poured a triple shot sans ice into a tumbler. My first drink in thirty days. Then, I watched and listened, hoping for the rumbling to cease. Mom's last breath escaped at 2:30 P.M. I called the mortuary to pick up the body. They buried Lidia a week later in front of a small congregation.

Expectations (Eulogy, Unedited 2014)

The theme of this eulogy is expectation: A belief that someone will or should achieve or do something; A feeling or belief about how good someone will be. Expectations are set for friends, children, spouses, parents, relatives, jobs, society, and the list goes on. When expectations are met or exceeded then there is a feeling of gratitude and self-fulfillment. When expectations are not met there will always exist an excuse by the person, who was supposed to meet the expectation, as to the why the expectation was not met. Excuses = failure to achieve which equals character incompetence. A simple process of logic.

My mom always set high expectations for herself, her family, and friends. She did not need a Master's

Degree nor a million dollars to understand what was expected of her to do for others. She made cookies and all sorts of food for a multitude of people without wanting anything in return. She always made sure that she continued to give and made sure that when she looked back on her life that she exceeded all expectations of others. She was ill with late stage liver disease for the last 10 years and I am pretty sure no one knew that except for me. She was given a short amount of time to live in 2004. She still tried her hardest and did the most she could do for others. Her ability to exceed expectations for others is what kept her alive and happy. She even exceeded the short time frame the doctors gave her in 2004.

The last 6 months were very difficult on her physically and emotionally. She still did try to do the most and best she could with limited abilities. Her strong drive was unbelievable and surreal. When it came time to step in with full force I did. People have been asking me for weeks if I'm ok or if I need anything or telling me that I need support etc. The reason why I do not need any support and I am ok is because I gave my mom 100%. I exceeded her expectations, which in turn, placed my mind and soul at ease. In hindsight my mom and dad were the same in that manner and so am I. I can look back and actually say I gave it my all physically and emotionally with no regrets or mistakes. Conscience clear and she is no longer suffering. I can assure you I was with her for her last breaths and telling her it will be ok. Expectation; A belief that someone will or should achieve or do something; A feeling or belief about how good someone will be.

Escaping to Neverland

The building facades located within the Rochester Business District on Lyell Avenue indistinguishable. Chimney stacks hissed and coughed, expunging the sulfuric remnants created within their mortar and metal lungs, towards the sunless sky. Jenny and Davey had walked almost two miles to Pop 'N' Go, the only bodega in the city selling *Scream Horror Magazine*.

"We got it, Davey. Isn't this awesome? We're going to be the coolest kids in school. Everyone will be hanging out with us and reading."

"Yeah, I'm excited. For once, people won't shun us."

As they exited the store, a group of boys in their late teens encircled the children, each hurling a jibe. "Are you a boy or a girl? Your friend is a fatty. He needs a diet. Both of you need to leave this city. You don't belong. Losers."

"Shut up, you immature morons. You're ugly and stupid."

Davey whispered, "I don't like this, Jenny. What are we going do?"

"Come on. Follow me. Run." The magazine they had saved for a year to buy fell from her grip and into a muddy puddle.

"I'm trying, Jenny. I can't go any faster. Maybe that guy is right and I'm too big."

"Stop it, Davey. Those bullies are jerks. Look! Up ahead. Let's go. I think we'll be safe in that place," she said panting.

She grabbed the rusted handle of the wooden door vandalized with a red X from top to bottom and yanked. Entering, a throbbing crowded her forehead, then encircled her throat. Hands iced and feet burning, she shivered, then stopped, leaning against the adjacent plaster wall layered with mold. Above her, two gargoyles affixed to the cathedral arch followed her into the building.

"Davey. Did you feel that?"

"What?"

"Forget it. Will you please hurry? Get inside."

Wheezing, he crashed into the door. "I'm here. I really need to exercise."

"Oh… give it a rest. Please. You'll have plenty of time for that."

"What's happening, Jenny?"

"I don't know. Nothing. I'm trying to find my breath like you. I'm not cold or hot anymore."

"What?"

"Never mind. Don't bother. Sometimes… I want to—"

Just as Davey dragged his battered sneaker across the plane of the entrance, the door slammed. Startled, he stumbled onto the gravel floor scraping his knees, then flopping onto his back. "Dammit, Jenny." He regained his composure. "Jenny… Jenny?" Silence not one of her attributes. Craning his head, he noticed the two, ceramic figures with glistening, ruby eyes espying his every move. He shuddered and blinked, but they didn't disappear. "Oh, no…," he mumbled.

Jenny stood awestruck at the center of the empty warehouse. He called to her again, but she didn't respond. A man as tall as three draped in a grey, spiraling overcoat, which flamed as it brushed his cement pedestal, nodded with surety. His enormous stovepipe hat immune to gravity.

Davey, cupping his face and crouching, peeked between the spaces of his tiny fingers and said, "Jenny... Jenny? What or who is that?" No response.

"Don't be afraid," said the figure, its face obscured. He extended a scarred hand towards Jenny. "Hello, child. My name is Homer. Welcome to Neverland. I'm glad you stopped to visit us."

Jenny hesitated, turning and scanning the perimeter, hoping to find Davey for support, but he'd vanished. She raised her hand with caution, retreating it several times before surrendering and extending it to his. "I guess... thank you, sir. I'm here with my friend." Davey appeared unannounced, brushing her shoulder and grinning. Surprised, her knees buckled, regaining stature from a magnificent balancing act on her heels.

"Hello, little boy. Glad you made it as well. Follow me. I'll give you a quick tour."

Davey slid his fingers around hers and murmured, "I'm scared, Jenny."

"Don't worry. I'm here with you. We're going to do this together." She tightened her grip on Davey with each cautious step behind Homer.

Homer twirled his arms in the air, the cuffs and sleeves clapping like flags during a windstorm.

Pointing in random directions he said, "My dear friends, look around. The floor turns from gravel to gold over yonder. We know it as the yellow, brick road that paved Dorothy's way to Emerald City. I prefer using cobblestone, but the author wouldn't listen to me. Further ahead, you'll come upon the meticulous, croquet garden where Alice met the Queen of Hearts in front of the white, rose tree. I always wonder, if that tree had been any other color, then Alice may never have existed." His throaty laughter gave way to a sly smirk.

"This is amazing, Jenny." She remained silent, although her wide, welling eyes told her tale. "Wow, Mister Homer, what else? Tell me," Davey implored. His prior fears exchanged for lavish intrigue.

"Don't be snippy, imp. Only, if you ask nicely."

"Okay... I'm sorry. Please, Mister Homer."

"Much better. Glad you asked. Cinderella is awaiting her carriage to transport her to the ball. Kitty-corner is Snow White who needs the prince to wake her from a deep slumber. Just beyond them, Peter Pan sprinkles fairy dust and flies like a fearless aeronaut amongst the Darling children. Tucked deep into a forest, Red Riding Hood skips down a dirt path to her grandmother's house. Oh, how I wish Red was a little less naïve. Life takes strange twists and turns, just like the ones which brought you both to me."

"When can we go explore, Mister Homer?" Davey asked.

"Soon, very soon, But—"

"But what, sir. When can we leave?" Jenny had regained her voice and with it came determination. The courage masking the jitters roiling inside her stomach.

"Well, Jenny. I was getting to that before you interrupted. You shouldn't be so rude. You'll be able to leave just as soon as both of you complete a few tasks for me." His broad smile revealed hundreds of teeth, some as sharp as knives, and others as dull as stone.

"That's not fair. What the he—"

"Now, now, Jenny. Remember what I told you both. Don't be rude! The ruder you are, the longer you'll stay. Perhaps, you may never leave."

"Beyond these beautiful landscapes are several fields needing an aggressive tilling and several more that must be reaped. Once those are completed by you and Davey, you'll be able to leave Neverland. If I approve, of course."

"Wait. What? That'll take forever," Davey and Jenny barked in unison.

"No need to fret, lads. Forever can be a day or a lifetime. The quicker you get to work, the sooner you can depart. I promise you'll get one hour a day, not one minute less or more, to enjoy the festivities within Neverland."

"Jenny... How are we going to get out of this mess?"

"Follow my lead."

Jenny marched forward, knees as high as her chin, towards Homer with Davey in tow, stopping within inches of the towering being. She pursed her lips and wound her leg, delivering a powerful strike to Homer's shin. Davey followed, booting the other.

Homer screeched as he fell backwards onto the floor.

"Let's go, Davey. Towards the door. Hurry."

She pushed with all her might but the door wouldn't budge. She screamed, kicked, and punched as did Davey, but to no avail.

"It's locked, my dear louses." Prone, he sprung onto his feet.

"What do we do now, Jenny?"

"I really don't know. I'm worried. Sorry."

"Well then, you ungrateful hellions. I will be adding time to your sentence," he roared, adjusting the cloak, whipping the flames at its base toward the children.

"I love you, Jenny," Davey said sobbing.

"Move. Now! Stop staring at each other. No frowning. You get what you deserve." He adjusted the jacket cuffs and waved them forward. "I'll follow and direct you to the final destination."

"I love you, Davey." She hung her head, shaking it with disbelief as she took the lead in their trek to the wastelands.

Freedom Weeps (An Anthem for Democracy)

Blood spews from punctured sores,
Lashings, slashings, bullets bored;
Flags flap half-mast, batons beat like a drum
Against the shields of evil,

Commanded like pawns by the clowns
Of a waning regime: they pause and charge,
Their boots shudder the earth,
The Innocents await; praying, kneeling, shivering,

Freedom Weeps.

Sirens wail behind a wall of tanks,
Engines roaring, bucking them forward,
Strangling any point of escape,
Batons raised overhead, they strike like sledgehammers;

Skulls crack, bones snap, skin tears;
Blood pools around the blameless bodies
Infused with the burning blacktop grease.
The Innocents shriek, howl, moan

For the pain today and hundreds of years afore,
Reverberating throughout alleyways,
Up towards the darkening sky,
They whimper, scream, plead,

Freedom Weeps.

The dead piled two-by-two,
The maimed claw to safety,
Fingers shredded, nails unseated,
The pavement unforgiving.

The batons have eased,
Replaced with a toxic downpour,
Bombs blast poisonous gas,
Grating lungs, strangling breath, burning tears,

Freedom Weeps.

There will be tomorrow, and the day after that;
Months, years, eternity,
The Innocents will continue to rise
With fists in the air and fervent strides

Justice sought, justice fought, justice obtained,
The Innocents will rise,
Regimes will fall;
The Innocents will rise
Destroying the cycle of their prior demise.

Freedom weeps, but no longer for sorrow.

The American Supermarket

We carted along the aisle,
I, an innocent child
Latched onto Mama's hand,
Scanning each package,
Fearing the towering shelves,
The letters familiar,
Their meanings foreign,
Attempting to verse them in our native tongue.

Up ahead, we were startled,
More so I than Mama,
A woman with arms like a Rembrandt,
Stilts for shoes, a skirt riding her hip,
Slammed her bare thigh against our cart,
"Go back to where you come from,
Speak English! You're in America… Goddamnit!"

Her breath peculiar, toxic fire,
I stumbled, nudging Mama to retire,
She caught the cart handle
Erect like a ballerina holding a shield,
Then mumbled a vulgarity, of which I heard once before.

We continued onward, Mama stern,
I turned, the woman wobbled
Clopping like a horse,
Bare ass quaking shelves,
Her hand raised, a middle finger unfurling an invisible
American flag.

The Willow Tree

"Johnny... Johnny Redlove," the security guard called towards the waiting room.

"Here. I'm here, sir."

His hand offered up a weak salute. That same salute much stronger two years ago while serving in the military. He received a general discharge under honorable conditions. Sergeant Strauss wanted a Bad Conduct Discharge, but after the general court reviewed the case, they decided to keep the punishment to a minimum. He was busted, high and drunk at five A.M., sleeping against a pole at the perimeter fence. The rumor around the base suggested the court didn't want to open a Pandora's box with Johnny because ranking officials could be implicated in a drug-smuggling ring.

Today, Johnny is getting discharged from another place, The Rochester New York Veteran Center. It's his third stint due to the judge's orders, which Johnny refers to as *tours*, although Kabul may have been easier than kicking the habits. This tour lasted ninety days. The weed and cocaine from his military days spiraled into meth and heroin as a civilian, leading to multiple arrests and sleeping on park benches when he wasn't in a jail cell.

"Johnny. Come on up. You need to sign the release."

The guard eyed Johnny and nodded for him to come to the checkout counter. Johnny hadn't noticed the guard in the last ninety days. Today, he stood out like a crack in a mirror. He wore dark camos unlike the others who blended with the bright white tiles and walls.

"On my way," he said monotone, spinning the hospital wristband. His unlaced military boots dragged, leaving a scuff mark every other step against the immaculate floor.

"Hey, Private. Pick up those boots."

He did as he was told, accustomed to obey and avoiding eye contact.

"Where do I sign?"

"I'm sure this isn't your first rodeo. Sign on the X," he said, handing the pen to Johnny.

"I have a question before signing. Have you been wearing those camos the whole time you've been here?"

"Yes, Private. I work here. This is what we wear. I hope you heal your mind on the outside."

Hurt my mind. Why did he say hurt my mind?

The guard pushed the release button under the counter, sounding an alarm. The double-pane doors crept open. He exited, heaving a duffel bag over his shoulder. That same duffel bag had been with him since the war. He'd hide liquor and drugs in its secret compartments as well as carry his belongings from stoop to park bench.

The beaming sun warmed Johnny's face as a brisk autumn wind shivered him. He cupped his brow, glancing around the parking lot for someone to welcome him: a friend, a family member, maybe an enemy, but none could be found. He hailed a cab parked at the corner of the lot.

"Take me to 1313 Elmwood Avenue. The Brickstone."

The cabbie nodded into the rearview. The engine roared as the tires chewed the pavement. The five-mile trip lasting only a couple minutes. He slipped the cabbie a twenty and trekked the elongated driveway to his childhood home, dodging two Range Rovers and a Lexus. The three cars certainly worth more than the house.

At the front door, a faint melody played throughout the home, perhaps Bach or Beethoven, maybe even Mozart. They all sounded the same to him. Give him Guns N' Roses or Metallica and he'd sing you the whole song, picking out the chords. Leaning, he peered through the stained-glass oculi but didn't see anyone.

"I'm not surprised," he mumbled.

He placed his duffel bag onto the concrete steps, stood tall, and rang the doorbell twice. He waited and no one arrived. He rang again, this time like Morse code. Still, no one answered. He shook his head, drooped his shoulders, and tapped a steady rhythm with his boot. With his patience fleeting, he tried again.

"I'm over this. To hell with these damn assholes."

With one swift motion, he picked up his bag. As he took two steps down the concrete stairs, the door opened.

"Hey, Johnny. Where *are* you going? Come back right this minute and give me a hug. Mommy has missed you."

She didn't dare step outside, opting to stand in the doorway waiting for Johnny to return. Good ole Karen Redlove had treated Johnny with that standoffish attitude since he could remember. Once, when he was nine, he gashed his left leg so bad the blood soaked his sock and pooled his brand new sneaker. Running frantically through that same entrance, his hysterical screams reverberated throughout the home and down the street. An unfazed Karen sat at the kitchen table sipping a vodka gimlet, probably her third of the day. Johnny begged her for help. She shook her head, grinned, and waved him away.

"Better take care of all that blood, little boy. Make sure you clean the floor and your sneakers. When you're done fixing yourself come and give mommy a hug. I need some loving today since your dad doesn't give it to me. Like I tell him, if I can't get love here, I'll find it elsewhere. That goes for you too, Johnny."

Good thing Dad, better known as Bernie Redlove to Mom or sometimes Bernard when she hated him, was in the upstairs office that day. He rushed down the steps, hugged Johnny, swept him into his arms, and darted to the bathroom to tend the wound. According to Bernard, the cut needed stitches but it was too late to go to the hospital. He wrapped ten layers of gauze around the wound and secured it with two types of tape: surgical around the gauze and duct tape on top of that. His work didn't stop there either. He mopped all the blood prints throughout the house and washed the bloodied clothes and sneaker. By the time Johnny was ready to hug mommy, she was sipping her seventh vodka gimlet, soon to be the eighth, and half asleep on the couch.

"Come on, Johnny. I'm not going to wait all day. My heating bill is going to cost thousands with this door open. You rang the doorbell like twenty times so get a move on. Must be important for you to be here."

If you don't kill the enemy in the willow tree, you will die.

Johnny regained his composure and entered. "It's about time you opened the door. All you had to do was pick me up. Was that too much to ask?"

"I've been home all day, so I suppose I could've but from where, one of your park benches?"

"No, Mom. Rehab at the Rochester VA. I left you twenty voicemails."

"Oh my…" Her hand rose over her heart. "I don't check voicemail very often, if ever. Texts are a better option."

"I don't own a cell phone."

"Maybe, we'll get you one soon."

As Johnny entered, she turned to shut the door and he caught a glimpse of her smirk in the oculi reflection.

"Next time, I'll send a car for you. One of those cabs. Make sure you tell the VA to send me a notice by mail or text in the future. Calling is just not a good option," she said, adjusting her hair in that same reflection.

Just as he dropped his duffel bag, the phone rang. She sprinted, pounding the travertine tile, slipping twice, almost falling, and lunged for the phone.

"Hello, this is Mrs. Redlove, also known as Karen. Hello… Hello… Damn telemarketers." She ended the call and mimed throwing the phone across the room. "Don't you just hate when people call and never say anything on the other end."

Johnny passed her, shaking his head, sneaking a peak at the archaic, voicemail box sitting next to the handset receiver. The blinking number showed zero voicemails. His chest tightened as he gulped the rising bile.

"Damn you, Mom. You'll never change." He sat at the dining room table, sliding one of the five ashtrays towards him. He swiped the zippo from his pocket and lit a cigarette.

"Huh? I never change. How about looking in the mirror, Son?"

"I have and I look just fine." He knew that was a lie, but no other responses came to mind. He blew out a plume of smoke. "Anyway, why don't you get me one of those vodkas you've been drinking all day?"

"I don't think that's a good idea, especially since you just left rehab. Starts with one, and before you know it, you're ten in the hole. Coffee or water?"

"Coffee." He immediately lit another cigarette after extinguishing the last one. "How's Dad?"

She placed two oversized mugs onto the table, filling them to the brim, and set aside the coffee pot. "I haven't talked to him," she said, sitting across from

Johnny. "It's been a few weeks, maybe months. I don't keep track anymore. Most of the time he's not here."

"Why is his Rover parked in the driveway?"

"Well…" She raised the mug to her lips as the steam fogged her glasses. "He went on a long road trip with a *friend*. They rented an RV or something. He left one morning out of the blue. I found a note taped to the fridge."

Not the first time Bernie left home. He and Karen fought frequently. His only way to deal with her was to escape. He left two days after securing Johnny's leg with duct tape. Perhaps the blood had scared him, or a more logical and devious reason existed. Sometimes he'd spend days at a hotel, and other times, he'd disappear for weeks, sneaking into the house during dawn. Karen in a drunken slumber, and Johnny on his way to school or getting high with friends. The rumor, which spread like wildfire throughout the neighborhood, was told to Johnny by his friend's mom. She said Bernie had fallen in love with a younger, sober version of Karen, twenty years younger to be exact. Great for Bernie, bad for Karen and Johnny, but at least he showed up once in a while.

"Leaving a note suits Dad. Does he know I was at the VA?"

"To be honest, Johnny, I didn't know you were in rehab, so he wouldn't know. Remember, I didn't get any of your voicemails."

"Right, Mom." He raised his mug and toasted with a fake smile. "You deserve the *Mom of the Year* award. You've earned it."

"Shut up, Johnny. I don't need this crap." Her flimsy fingers rolled the flint of the lighter several times before igniting a flame for her cigarette. She rose up from the chair, exchanging the coffee mug for a rocks glass filled with vodka and lime. "See what you do to me, Johnny. I can't even enjoy my coffee."

"Oh… I bet you'll enjoy the vodka more. Pour me one, so I can enjoy it with you."

"Stop asking me. I can't and won't." She took a sip and flashed a gum smile with yellowing teeth.

Vodka clears the mind, cleans the soul. Vodka kills the mind, burns the soul.

"Pour me one. Now!" He slammed his fists onto the table. A lit cigarette jumped from the ashtray and rolled towards the centerpiece as coffee dribbled from the brim of the bouncing mug.

Karen stumbled and gasped, the gimlet glass almost slipping from her hand. Her cigarette fell onto the floor and under the fridge grate. "What the—what the hell, Johnny. You stop acting like that. Right this second. I'll call the damn police if I have to."

Johnny's glossed, hazelnut eyes rolled. He pinched the cigarette from the table and took a drag. "I'm sorry. I didn't mean it. Sometimes I can't control my reactions."

She gulped her drink and rushed to light another smoke. "It's fine. Don't let it happen again under my roof. Did the doctors even talk to you about your PTSD while you were in rehab?"

"Sometimes," he said, focusing on the rising steam from the mug. He had become accustomed to the calm before and after the storm but could never deal with the hurricane between. "I suppose they try to help, but it's hard to fix a broken mind."

The doctors never understood anything. Johnny tried explaining the storms many times; the stabbing needles rolling over his brain, each nodule bursting like bombs filled with shrapnel. Then, the throbbing commenced, followed by a trickling around his skull.

He'd search his hair and massage his scalp, but never could find the blood.

"They want me to take meds, but I don't want them. The meds make you a zombie. You can't feel and sometimes you can't even hear."

"Maybe you should listen to the doctors. Then, you won't have these episodes anymore."

"Everything is always easier said than done."

"I have a great idea, Johnny." She tipped her glass for a quick sip. "I think you should go to the lake house. Take some *me* time. Looking at the waves will calm and clear your mind."

"I guess that's an option. Can't hurt, right?" He shrugged while a puff of smoke billowed from his mouth.

"I'll drop you off later tonight. I need to run a couple errands. Just hang out. Take a nap. The bed's made in your old bedroom. Nice and comfy."

"Okay. Sounds like a plan. I'll chill and rest. I'll be ready when you return."

Karen left with the speed of cheetah, screeching the tires at the base of the driveway. Johnny emptied the last of the coffee into the sink, rinsed the mug, and placed it onto the marble countertop. Just as he returned to his seat at the table, the phone rang, which he ignored. On the eighth ring the voicemail recording clicked on:

"Hi. You've reached Karen. Please leave a voicemail. I'll be quick to return your call." The caller obliged. "Hello, Karen. This is the Rochester VA. This is a follow-up to our prior voicemails. We released Johnny to your care per his instructions today. Sometimes our enrollees have a hard time adjusting to their first free day. If you notice any odd or violent behavior, please call us or 911. Have a great day."

The voicemail flashed the number "one." Johnny wasn't going to have any VA balderdash disrupt his flow. He hit the delete button.

"To hell with the VA. I need some fresh air."

At the front door, he paused with his hand on the handle. Children outside screamed and laughed. The kids always had parents nearby and those people frightened him. If they spotted him, a barrage of questions followed: "How have you been, Johnny? Are you feeling better? Anything new? Thank you for your service, Johnny. I wish I could've served. How was the war, Johnny?" And so on and so on.

He locked the door and tramped to the three-car garage. He scanned the empty space, took a deep breath, and slid out a cigarette. When young, he spent most of his free time in the garage. An odd but comforting solace emanated from the enclosure. The violent arguments between Mom and Dad never penetrated the walls, and without disruption, he could smoke weed and drink liquor. Those were the days, and these days, well, these days are more tiresome and less fun.

He traced the edges of the painted, oak shelves and pine countertops, which were supposed to be workbenches. Those were for show, of course, because Dad couldn't even bandage a leg, let alone build something. Mom, after the seventh vodka, would saw her arm off. He remembered stashing a bunch of liquor and drugs on a shelf abutting the top, rear corner of the wall. He hoped no one had ever found them.

He leveraged his boot at the bottom and hoisted himself upward. The process not as fast as when he was young. At the top, he slithered his hand around papers and bubble wrap. With his arm buried deep inside, he nudged and pushed, then without notice, two bottles wrapped in rope fell, crashing against his nose and cheek. Behind them, an ounce of weed, a filled pill bottle, and a blue baggie filled with powder.

Vodka numbs the mind. Whiskey makes it clear. Do not fear.

He climbed down smiling, his first one of the day, with the treasure tucked against his chest. He surveilled the surroundings as if someone had seen him take the goods, but the coast was clear. He ran into the home, returning to the garage with the duffel bag, and stuffed it.

Great job, Johnny. You deserve a rest. Or a drink.

Throwing the bag over his shoulder, he marched to the bedroom upstairs. To his surprise, Mom hadn't changed the room's interior since he moved out after graduating from high school. A Guns N' Roses poster hung above the bed next to Aerosmith, and on the other walls, various models from Maxim and Playboy, as well as Nirvana and NIN prints illuminated by a lava lamp. Affixed to the black ceiling, hundreds of stars, which glowed in the darkness; each one glued by hand during a drunken stupor. The comforter and the sheets the same as well, imprinted with animal shadows. He slipped off his boots and dropped the bag onto the worn carpet.

He thought about uncapping a liquor bottle, but decided against the notion, sliding it under the covers and closing his eyes. Not too long after he sank into a deep slumber, his eyes zigzagging under wavering eyelids. He found himself calm, flanked by sand and lush vegetation, gazing at the sky, then a mortar exploded.

"Hey! Private Redlove. Are you okay?" asked Sergeant Strauss, nicknamed SS by the platoon.

"Yeah. I'm fine. Is everyone else okay?"

"I think so, but we have a problem, JR. Two Taliban just bolted into the brush up ahead. Go in there and find them. Kill at will, Private. Do you copy?"

"Yes, Sergeant. I'll track 'em. Damn Taliban."

Johnny rose from a push-up and trooped towards the brush. A thick willow stood front and center, skirted by waist-high bushes. Behind them, towering palms swayed with each wind gust. As he approached the willow tree, he noticed faint movement between the low-hanging branches. A quick glance over his shoulder showed no backup. He created a path using the tip of the gun barrel and entered with caution. Once breached, he found himself within arm's length from a child who couldn't have been more than ten or twelve. The child attempted to run.

"Hey! Halt. Now. Do—not—move." He raised the M4 Carbine.

The child didn't respond but stopped with one hand tucked into a chest pocket, and the other dangling towards his thigh.

"Little boy. Take your hand out of your pocket. Please. Hand." Johnny pointed at his hands, then the child's, hoping sign language could resolve the issue. "Remove." He knew if the boy had an explosive belt, they'd both be dead.

"Me. No. Me. No. Please. Thank you. No, me. Me, no," he said quavering, eyes fearful.

"I don't understand, kid. Show me your hand. Take it out of your pocket. We don't want anything bad to happen to either of us. We both want to live." Johnny offered a cautious smile and continued to demonstrate a vague, hand-pulling gesture.

"Me. No—me. Please," he said cowering. His welling eyes brought a stream of tears soaking his soiled thobe. "No, me. No me. Thank you. Please. No—no."

Johnny's finger trembled atop the trigger, his eyes affixed to the boy's pocketed hand, beads of sweat dribbling into his eyes, pooling upon his upper lip. He steadied the barrel while his other hand wiped his brow. At that very moment, the boy's linen wiggled. Johnny freaked, discharging the weapon, unleashing one deafening shot. The boy flumped to the ground, blood pooling around his head, eyes open. Johnny threw the gun, rushed to his side, and knelt.

"Wh—what have I done?"

He panted, caressing the boy's bloodied hair. His hand, unfazed by the gunshot, had remained in the pocket. Johnny, certain to find a detonator attached to a bomb, cautiously removed it from the thobe.

"I'm sorry, little boy," he said with a guttural wail as he held the boy's hand gripping prayer beads. Johnny folded the boy's small arms across his chest and rolled his eyelids closed. A barreling wind soon followed thrusting Johnny to the ground, blinding him with sand. He awoke, startled by snapping branches and scattering rocks.

"What the hell have you done, Private?" SS bellowed.

"I don't know, sir." He shook his head, then cleared the grime from his eyes. "I don't know. I'm sorry, sir."

"You killed a child. What the fuck is wrong with you, Private? There's going to be hell to pay. Get up and get back to camp. I'll try to fix this mess."

Johnny found himself huddled next to the perimeter fence, his fingers dangling through the gaps, attempting to escape.

"Wake up, Johnny. Rise and shine. It's time to get up and go."

"What? Who?" His eyelids fluttered, then opened.

"It's Mom. I'm back. Better get ready for the lake house."

The willow tree. The willow tree. It sees you, does it see me?

He rolled from bed, slipped on his boots, and headed to the bathroom to freshen up. The dream had taken much of the energy sleep was supposed to provide. A rinse of mouthwash, he accidentally swallowed, brought him some reprieve, and a splash of cold water to his face woke him just enough to acquire a glimpse into the mirror. Pillow creases carved his face and scratches stretched from his forehead to his neck in the reflection. He thought back to the dream, concluding the scrapes must've occurred while he breached the willow tree. The only problem, the tree couldn't harm him in a dream. He shrugged, followed by another dose of mouthwash he gleefully swallowed, and plodded downstairs.

"Hey, sleepy head. Are you feeling better?" Mom said, filling a cup with vodka and ice.

"I guess. The military taught us sleep doesn't always mean rest. Maybe the lake house will be more relaxing."

"What happened to your face?"

"Nothing. I think I scratched myself in a dream."

"More like a nightmare, Johnny. Get some Neosporin and Band-Aids."

"Whatever. Are you ready to take me?"

"Yes. Just give me a few minutes to finish this drink. I'm parched and stressed from doing errands." She gulped and set the glass down with a hint of fury as if her petty life was more stressful than his.

"Fine. I'll be in the garage waiting."

He lit a cigarette and strolled the shelving as he had done earlier. One cigarette led to three, thinning what little patience he had.

"Come on. Are you ready yet? Let's get this over with." Hanging out at his childhood home drummed up too many bad memories. The silence even worse.

"I'm ready. Boy, let me tell you, I really needed that drink." She swayed through the doorway. "We're taking the black Rover."

"Finally." He squashed the butt under his boot.

He followed her to the truck. The passenger door opened without a key, starting the vehicle in the same manner. Expensive options for the wealthy would've helped the platoon's Humvee in Kabul. The drive commenced towards Lake Ontario. Johnny steadfast and staring straight ahead, hypnotized by the harvest moon showcasing its naked imperfections and burning the sky red like a setting sun.

"Wake up. We're here. A getaway like a spa day." She slammed the shifter into park, opened the glovebox, and pulled out a mini vodka among the twenty or so bottles crammed into the compartment.

"Good. This is better than your place."

"It can be." She took a swig and unlocked the door. "I used to come here quite a bit to get away from your father."

Built in the fifties, the one bedroom cottage, two if the makeshift wall divided by a curtain is included, resembled a doll house next to the extravagant homes surrounding it. Weathered oak trusses, ripened by the harsh winters and warm summers, crisscrossed the ceiling. She toggled the light switch until the filaments from the low hanging bulbs sparked and warmed, illuminating the aging, pine floor.

"Make yourself at home. Call me if you need anything." Before he could respond, she gulped the remnants of vodka and darted to the truck.

He dragged a twine chair from the nearest wall and placed it ahead of the sole table centered in the cottage. He set the duffel bag at his feet. One hand caressed the waving crevices of the chiseled circle of wood built decades ago and no wider than an arm, as the other sparked a cigarette. He scanned the room and inhaled. The brief silence soothed his mind, interrupted by a rickety screen slapping the rear door. He took a long drag from the cigarette, sighed, and went to inspect the noise. Gusts of wind had loosened the jerry-rigged straps and screws keeping it in place. He tried to deal with the nuisance sans any tools or know-how and failed.

Straight ahead, Lake Ontario provided respite, reflecting the rising moon battling the thickening clouds. Sporadic flashes in the distance suggested an imminent storm would win their war. In the backyard and to the right stood a domineering willow tree of which he never recalled existing. Its lush foliage like the mane of a lion. As it swayed, its center formed eyes and the branches twisted, creating a nose and pursing lips.

Willow tree. Willow tree. Do you see me? I see you. Willow tree. Willow tree.

He turned, slammed the door, and smacked the bar lock closed. With his hand resting upon the jamb, he wondered when the willow tree had been planted. Something that mammoth couldn't be missed. The more he thought, the more the discussion rambled. Trees exist everywhere, except deserts. This isn't a desert. Perhaps, he'd never looked at the corner of the yard. After two deep breaths, he decided best not to deal with it tonight. The debate had pinnacled. He needed rest and relaxation at the lake house, not arboriculture studies.

He leaned back on the twine chair and stretched his arms towards the ceiling, tracing a support beam in the air with his fingertips. Its ridges and notches carved by a chisel rather than weather. Extending his legs, he kicked the duffel bag onto its side. Two bottles thumped onto the floor. He placed them onto the table and unraveled the snug rope, measuring more than ten feet. He pulled it taut and remembered why he had tied it to the bottles. It was the same rope he and Dad used to pull his wagon up and down the street. The good ole days when the Redlove household lived within the confines of happiness. Those days now long gone.

The bottles kept leering at him like the willow tree. Stern and mighty with their colorful labels calling his name. *Johnny. Johnny. Come taste me, Johnny.* The remnants from the mouthwash tingled his throat, returning the pleasant memories he spent with a bottle of liquor. The good ole days when drinking hard went unaffected. Rehab taught him to take it easy, so he knew he'd be fine.

Just one, maybe two, or three, but no more than four.

From the cupboard, he retrieved a tumbler and set it upon the table. Rocking back and forth in the chair, he whirled the glass like a spinning top. It beckoned to be filled by its masters. *Just one, maybe two, or three, but no more than four.* He obliged and twisted the cap from the vodka bottle, filling the glass to the brim. One sip, two sip, three, and the glass emptied. He refilled it with whiskey from the other bottle. One sip, two sip, three. The lighter's flame struggled to find its paper target, singeing part of his five o'clock shadow.

"Damnit. For fuck's sake."

On reflex, he kicked the duffel bag, spilling the baggie and pill bottle onto the floor. He scooped them and dumped the contents onto the table, raking each pill into similar-colored piles. Wobbling hands grasped two pills from each, chasing them with a shot of liquor. A sense of calm intertwined with a tingling of happiness swarmed his body as his eyes darted.

A writhing snake appeared upon the edge of the table. Lunging for it, he grabbed it on the first attempt, surprising himself with the accuracy of a cat. As he pulled it towards him, he realized it wasn't a snake, just the rope he'd used to secure the bottles of liquor for storage.

Lightning shimmered through the windows, followed by a boom that shook the cottage and his sternum. A howling wind ensued, snapping the loosened screen against its wooden frame like a whip. Hesitant to rise at first, he decided best to address the noise or his buzz would be ruined. He peered through the rear window checking for damage, then opened the door, but neither provided visibility into the blackness. Caterwauling gales demanded the waves clobber the shore. A bolt of lightning struck the ground several feet away, numbing his tongue and prickling his skin. As the flashbulbs dissipated from his eyes, a towering flame appeared.

Willow tree. Willow tree. Do you see me? I see you.

Engulfed, the willow tree. Its eyes wide and piercing, nostrils flaring, mouth grazing the ground and screaming, the branches bunching and forming hundreds of fangs.

Willow tree. Willow tree. Time to come visit me.

Johnny stood mesmerized. The tree then morphed once again. Its eyes melted, replaced with skeletal sockets. Its nose fell to ash upon the ground and its lips burst into papier-mâché. The fangs multiplied to a thousand daggers. Inside the jaw, the body of the child from Kabul, lying in that same pool of blood with his eyes open.

Johnny. Johnny. The willow tree wants to see you. Please come quick.

The wind charged inside the cottage, jolting the table and strobing the lights. He grabbed the twine chair, and with a stern grip, centered it under the same support beam he had eyed earlier. He cleared the bottles and drugs from the table, leaving only the rope behind.

Wrap it right. Wrap it tight.

He laid it out forming three esses. One part remained limp as the other two fell into his stronghold like rosary beads. Seven times he wound the rope around its center. Seven deadly sins, seven trumpets, seven heavens with the seven seals. He flung the rope over the beam and tied it taut. The noose slid over his head and onto his neck like a scarf. He counted to seven, kicked the chair from under his feet, then his neck snapped.

Welcome to the willow tree, Johnny.

National Suicide Prevention Lifeline

If you are suicidal, thinking about hurting yourself, or are concerned that someone you may know may be in danger of hurting themselves, Please Call 1.800.273.TALK (8255).
https://suicidepreventionlifeline.org

For TTY Users: Use your preferred relay service or dial 711 then 1.800.273.8255.

Veterans 1.800.273.8255, then Press 1 or Text 838255.
https://www.veteranscrisisline.net

All services are confidential.

SAMHSA's National Helpline

SAMHSA – Substance Abuse & Mental Health Services Administration.

Please Call 1.800.662.HELP (4357).
TTY: 1-800-487-4889

SAMHSA's National Helpline is a free, 24/7, 365-day-a-year, treatment referral and information service (in English and Spanish) for individuals and families facing mental and/or substance use disorders.

https://www.samhsa.gov

All services are confidential.

About the Author

Thank you for reading. I'm flattered as well as grateful. This will not be the "typical" about-the-author page.

I lived in Rochester, NY for most of life, then moved to the Cape Coral / Fort Myers, FL. This is my second book. If you've made it to the end, then you know the themes in this book vary from love to death and everything between. I opted not to include any blurbs about each piece because I want the reader to interpret the poems and short stories. We can save my meanings for a future Q & A.

If you like horror, please check out *Stained Mirror*, which is available at all outlets.

On writing: I hope to have additional novels out soon. They will not be limited to any genre.

My online information:
www.giannifranco.com, Twitter: @giannipetitti,
    IG: gianni.franco, FB (love/hate): Author Gianni Franco, for now. May delete again.